Milk Tooth
Martha Sprackland

after all you could have lived out your life with bare floors and furniture, or with sealed windows and doors...

—Judith Jarvis Thomson, *A Defence of Abortion*

A room in London

What do I remember? My roommates: the sanguine one
in bed to my left, hair in a ponytail, reading Joan Didion,
and the one to my right, smaller
even than me, who held up her hand
with its abstract of blood after the misoprostol
like she had the answer to a question at school
and the nurse came over with something for the sickness.
That room was like a lighthouse, very bright, very quiet.
I could've been there several hours or several days
while my mother circled the building in her car
or ate a pastry at the café across the street—
I have never asked. I had countless mugs of sugary tea,
an ache, a ferrous tongue, and then an orderly struggling to hold
my shoulders like the handles of a pneumatic drill
as she told me urgently what I already knew—
that *it's already done*   *it'll be much worse for you now if you don't.*
The pattern and weight of a cotton gown, at least, in pastel blue
       and green.
Our little beds, bars of autumnal light falling through the curtains.

Sentiment

The life you had is nothing. It is the life you have that is important.
—Jeanne Moreau

This motto is described as *fastidiously unsentimental*
though of course this is incorrect:
we are most sentimental about nothings.

During the interview
she ate a large quantity of meat.

Some children I have met
are very beautiful. Not all, of course;
some children are imbeciles, vulgar, terrible.

I would like to write a wonderful utopia
for my breasts to live in,
a paradise—

(I feel guilty for late development
that they budded and bloomed
and were flyblown so soon).

It's true that I buried things in the garden
that might've lived
a little longer.

Life is risking! Sure
but tell that to this pile of splintered wood.

It was wonderful there, she said of her village,
every tombstone in the cemetery was for a Moreau.

Goodbye, school holiday
lousy with sunlight.

Goodbye, nothing!

Lineage

We decided to have the abortion, became killers together.
—Sharon Olds, *The End*

We two conspired to cut the cord
and truncate the female line
at the cusp of its execution.

How can I write about what I can't remember?
The lights are down in that dark theatre.
I imagine that we met in shady corners of the house
like mobsters, away from the males.

It was a matter of survival.
She must have seen approaching the fatal fear
that took my equilibrium for years,
and claimed it as her duty.

We didn't know yet how we would do it,
by exile, by knife, by blood,
by money. Always,
my part of the bargain was to forget.

Gibbet

Song for anaesthesia

There was a row of objects hanging
from the railing by coloured ribbons.
It was a lovely muddy morning,
riven with reflective tracks,
clouds clumping in the hedgerows.
To the left of the lane, hemlock
jouncing gaily on its stems, to the right
cow parsley shoving and shouldering.
There was a balloon tied to the barbed wire,
its red skin pulled tight, swollen,
squeaky fat lip, translucent,
and a number of others worked loose,
floating up, off into that clean
wet waking field. Hooks through
their mouths, tails trailing, they moved
away across the slowly filling
prints and runnels of the sky.

Gates

A shut family, a five-year plan, is so vital.
There is a mummy of conversation,
a mummy place online—
Gravitate, you lovely things, you aches!
We are not two friends. We are a children tribe.
Listen—children are in boxes.
Advertisement. Kitchen tears
down the middle. *Advertisement.*
Sadly, sadly, sadly literature on the subject.
Anyway they increasingly had suitcases, the friends,
had dinners and Septembers and we
an afterthought. So much of mothering
happens at the gates. An *interior* afterthought.
Our divorced decades, stretching down the road
in front, are exactly as we envisaged! The open road.
Gates opening and closing like valves
to breath. Talk sweetly, old friend, surprise me.
Clusters of mummy, like blood.

Still life with rotted tooth

In the thick glazed bowl, red apples
perch in an ambassadorial pyramid

a napkin of sunlight is unfolded
on the wooden table

and there is a secret gleam of silver
on the handle of the knife

that cut the apple into thick quarters
each with a shocked rind of skin

around the pale flesh. Three quarters
stop untouched at timepiece angles

on a green ceramic plate, next to a splayed book
pages folded uncomfortably. To the fore

the tooth lies like a letter-opener, just-used
its taproot pointing to the window

its blackened face a fly-hole
and inside the tooth

the maggot of the fly

Abstract

The white-bearded doctor
swung the monitor to face me (unthinkable
that they would do that now)
and abruptly began to speak—
lo digo, es imposible que no sabías.
No sabía. I hadn't known.
Even then, appraising
the television's weird sketch
I was the uninitiated at the gallery
the night the work goes up
and tried to think of something to say
to the old artist who waited, expectant,
about his challenging new abstract
in sugar-paper, collage text and chalk.

Speculum

I recognise you jabbing
at the lawn with your muscular beak.
Rapacious curve

corvid invader, your searching pocks the earth
between the wet grass stems,
delves in derelict logs, raiding the soil

for what, Raven? You ratchet apart
those cold bill-halves, scissorlike
with their strikefear *cleck*

and rive the ground's dark
for things that shine, for things that crawl
damply through their burrows

blind unsuspecting things and pale.
Dead blue bird, you lie at hand
empty as a plague-mask.

Taxes

There is a state in which
the tumourous body has wonderful skin

The miracle of cesspits, how lush their sickly lips
so athrob with vigour it's like a little Eden

The sess is unavoidably levied on the cells
but you seem fine, they say

A tax, a maggoty apple
is a fact of life

Some burning houses
have beautiful windows

Twilight Sleep

The next thing I knew I was awake, and I heard the sympathetic voice of Dr Krönig saying 'All ees well', and then I thought to myself 'I wonder how long before I shall begin to have the baby,' and while I was still wondering a nurse came in with a pillow, and on the pillow was a baby, and they said I had had it—perhaps I had—but I certainly can never prove it in a courtroom.

—The Truth About Twilight Sleep, New York Times, 31 January 1915

Like a diamond ring in cushioned velvet. They show how it mewls when slapped, how its eyes crack, the jailer's torchlight flickering past the keyhole of the prison door. What a sleepy baby. Krönig rests his foot on the clouds, steps out onto them. *Have I showed you this before?* The buds of the ovaries at the finials of their elegant branches, the pear-shaped space they come to. The baby curls and uncurls cloudily on its mount. *What is this, what does this do*, he asks, close to my face. I know it is a way of looking inside, or of bringing-forth. Time is like blood, pulsing and pausing, loosing clots. What is the tool, arms like the fork in a plant with sweet black berries? Krönig lectures on the far-famed storks of Frieburg, on the modern irrelevance of pain. *If there is no memory of pain, it is equivalent to having had no pain, and a doctor then certainly has the right to speak of 'painless childbirth'.* I am glad that this diadem is here, under glass, next to the scalpel, the silver thread. The remembering-game again! The wishbone is in the doctor's hand. The clouds are clotting across the sky of my mind. Ah. It is his stethoscope. *The benefits of twilight sleep, madam: a lift in the birth rate. A lift in the marriage rate, as the fear of the torture accompanying motherhood is lifted. The preservation of youth and beauty through the removal of agony.* It is a pair of forceps. The baby walks in through the door, a golden cuckoo, fully grown, carrying a bowl of sand on a silken pillow. I sleep another five hours. I am in my pleasant swaddling of clouds. An instrument is held out on its velvet cushion. Krönig speaks: *Do you know what this is? Have I showed you this before?*

Gasoline

Als ich vom Himmel fiel

When I pass a petrol station and catch
the hot stink of orange peel, vomit,
coriander, turpentine, grass, I think
involuntarily of Juliane Koepcke
walking through the Peruvian jungle for eleven days,

pouring gasoline on her skin
to draw the maggots out. I remember that she counted
thirty-five worms, that her mother Maria hung
strapped to an aeroplane seat in the canopy
for three days before dying.

On the other hand,
Annette Herfkens survived over a week
after her plane crashed in Vietnam.

I breathe the ruined air in, breathe it out,
compute the extent of their injuries.

Pulpo

In the supermarket upturned octopuses
lie on stones of ice as on a cold beach
or an operating table. Obscene, as they should be
with their legs splayed, their underside
slick soft-blush as a cunt.
Their anonymity is correct,
that they can turn over onto their back
and be examined under market lights,
their petite grasping suckers
undulating, pulsing, picking up and
dropping the clicking chips of ice.

Tooth

Like a round grey stone lodged
in the fork of a tree
the tooth sits intractably
at the far back of the mouth
between the ear and the jaw.

The mouth can't close fully,
like a freezer door;
can't crank itself open
more than a few gear-teeth's width,
enough for water through a straw.

At night it wakes up
like an eyeball, lolls sourly on the tongue
rolls against the drum
tampers with the hinge
and rubs it raw.

Nothing to do, between the shift-
change of the painkillers
but listen to my bedmate
breathing asleep and the foghorns
in the hot harbour.

All the world's cameras
are on this clamorous point:
this knot, this bole, this clot,
this breaking news, this fire,
this prisoner of war,

a sealed world seething
like a black egg
incorruptible by amoxicillin
and saline wash.
I want it out.

I go down to the dockside,
oily between the cruise ships
and Maersk containers,
to gargle palmfuls of the sea
against the hard bezoar

and its faulty magic.
I idle towards
the half-bottle of whiskey,
the red-handled relief
in the kitchen drawer,

but Ed shifts and turns against me,
skin like cotton, outside the pain,
and says through sleep—
his clean sound mouth—
Honey, are you still sore?

I can't answer
round the cobblestone,
the ship, the choke, the pliers,
the acorn cracked
and pushing through the floor.

Milk

I came back to Moratalaz
at the season's close, bombed
with knockout drugs

of my own tricked body's making
(as the blinded bird on the Rastro is duped
into its troublous & unhappy song).

Dime, cielo, the waitress asked
as she moved outlying tables from the reach
of a smartly bruising sky.

In the nights I leaned against the walls,
dragged my shoulder along them
not crying, not making a noise, walking

through a factory wastefully producing chemicals.
She was patient. *Dime, cielo—*
*Tell me—*and finally I went with her

out into the plaza and the beginning rain
the swollen water darkening
the pale, dry shirt of stone.

De la lycanthropie, transformation et extase des sorciers

A fourteen-year-old girl named Haxti was in 1838 the last child-sacrifice of the Pawnee Morning Star ritual.

The last wolf in England was killed in the early sixteenth century, though they were to be found in Scotland, in the forests of Braemar, until 1684.

Haxti dreams of a slatted forest of pines　like slits in hide
the sift and spin　of leaf-litter lifting with a breeze
and settling　over the tops of her calf-boots

there is a word for the way in dreams motion　breaks
and splinters into refracted light　a staggered sequence
of disparate pictures　a slowing-down zoetrope

imagine a falcon wheeling and dropping on the wing
imagine the perfect circle drawn　by its outer pinion
it is impossible　that this image is steady

or the bird's flight　compass-clear
in Haxti's dream the needles fall from the trees　in stages
the light is of standing　inside a sheaf of corn

/

two hundred years ago　in Braemar　she runs with hunters
her hair shorn as a boy
hung about with pheasant　and gibbet-traps

like leaf-motes　in a coil of wind　they gather
in diminishing circles around the wolf
its red tongue lolling in concentration

the traitor earth   pushing against the flight
the arrow further entering the breast
when they draw the knife   and let the hot blood out

Haxti crosses herself   swears allegiance to the king
as she does to the compass-point
now all other arrows   find a mark

/

wolf-thoughts   a fever-dream
these people the Chahiksichahik know
tskirirara   from *tski-ki*   from wolf-in-water

the *loupe*   the strangers who keep her as she sleeps
in the shattered forest the sacred wolf   lopes through pine trees
through the series of half-open doors   until the last   springs shut

in the daylight hours they feed her well
tell her the creation stories   in which she has her part
that the wolf was the first animal to know death

Haxti dreams of the past   the images overlapping
like leaves on the forest floor
she was brought here to sleep

/

France in winter   a black night
flocks of birds fly   jerkily   over the fields
where the shepherds   black with hunger

have savaged their own flocks   and
children   the flesh eaten from their thighs
by the *loup-garou* Gilles Garnier   the hermit

who made a deal with the spirit of the forest
in the grip   of hunger and   burned
on the scaffold as a man   though the meat

smelled like dog   what human jaws
could cut a boy in two at the belly
a bird   circles the stake for the carrion

/

the appearance of the morning star
the resin-torches dipped into the fire   the resin clubs
all touched to Haxti's legs and arms

there are no forests   in the Badlands
where they lose the last girl-child
the priest holds the dried meat ready

they were kind   it is the Wolf who leads her   to the sacrifice
when the arrow comes into her heart
she scatters   her own fire

once all males of the tribe   have loosed their bows
and she is full of needles   and the ash is cool
Haxti is taken down and made again to sleep

/

the simplest of all the dreams
is full of still   and full of quiet
the wolf's huge head   rests   in her lap

she speaks   the creation myth
of the wolf who let the humans into the world
and who was killed by them   at the Fall

there is a word   for the way   in dreams   motion   breaks
and splinters into   refracted light   a staggered sequence
of disparate pictures   a slowing-down   zoetrope

two   broken arrows   lie to the side   two black feathers
slowly   the pine needles   fall   and   cover them
all   the forest's doors   are open